MOUSE IN LOVE

by Robert Kraus

illustrated by

Jose Aruego and
Ariane Dewey

SCHOLASTIC INC.

New York Toronto London Auckland Sydney
Mexico City New Delhi Hong Kong

ISBN 0-439-27135-5

12 11 10 9 8 7 6 5 4 3 2 1   1 2 3 4 5 6/0

Printed in the U.S.A.   24

First Scholastic printing, February 2001

Book design by Mina Greenstein. The text of this book is set in 24 point Futura Medium.
The illustrations are ink, watercolor, and pastels.

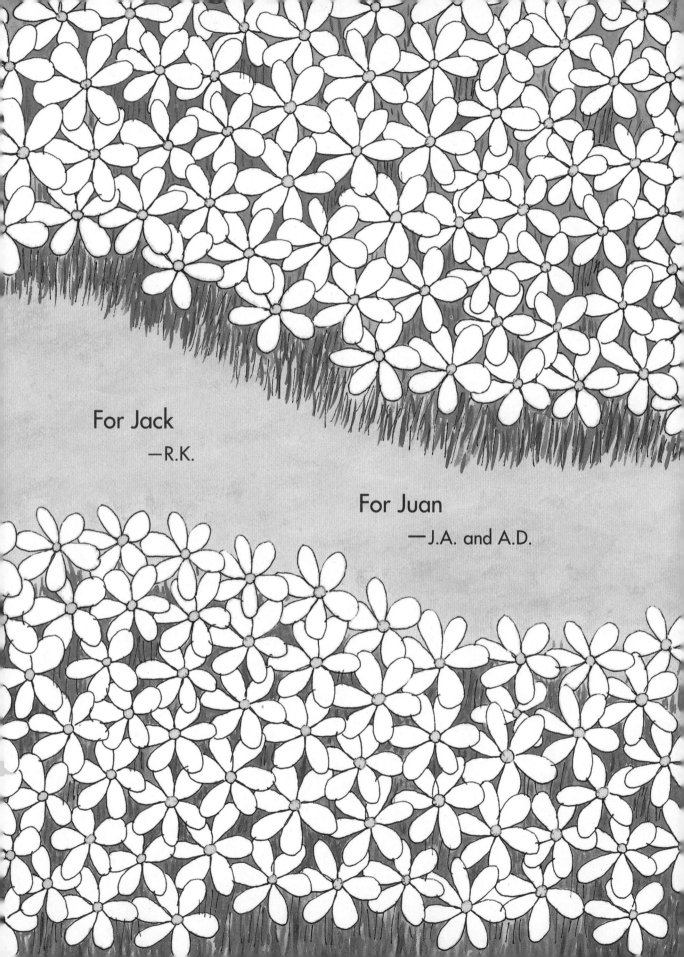

For Jack
—R.K.

For Juan
—J.A. and A.D.

She loves me.
She loves me not.
She loves me.

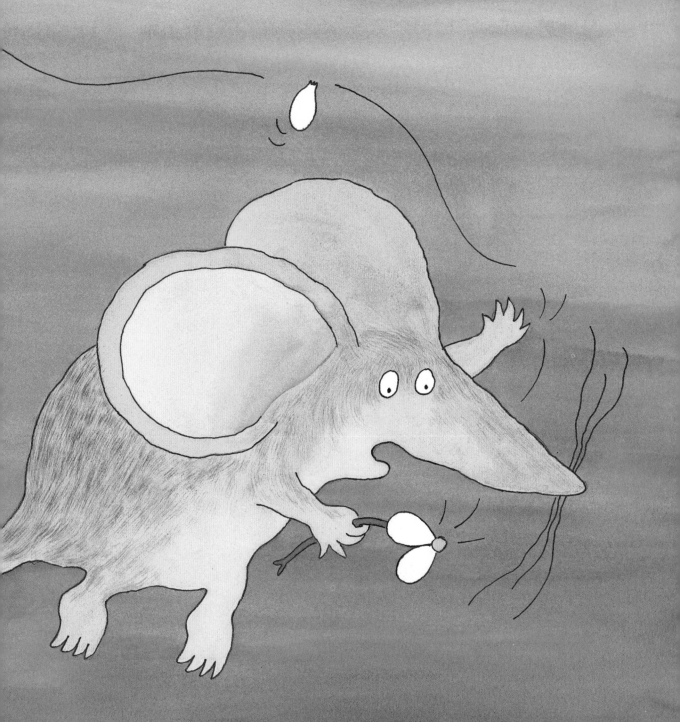

She loves me not.

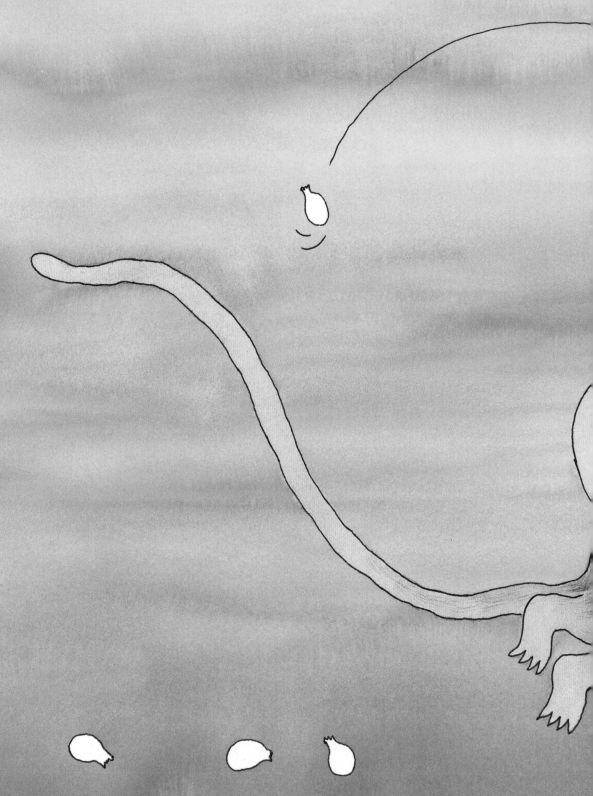

She loves me!

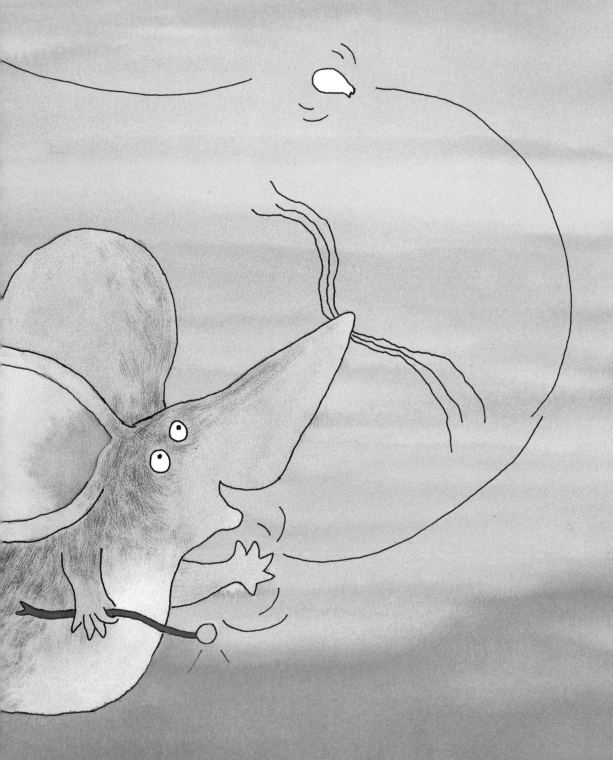

"Why so dreamy, little mouse?"

"I'm in love!"

"Who's the mouse?"

"She's the mouse of my dreams.
I've never met her.
But try as I may, I can't forget her."

"So what will you do?"

"Look for that mouse
and try to get her."

"Where will you find her?"

"Maybe she waits in a palace fine."

"Maybe she waits at the end of the line."

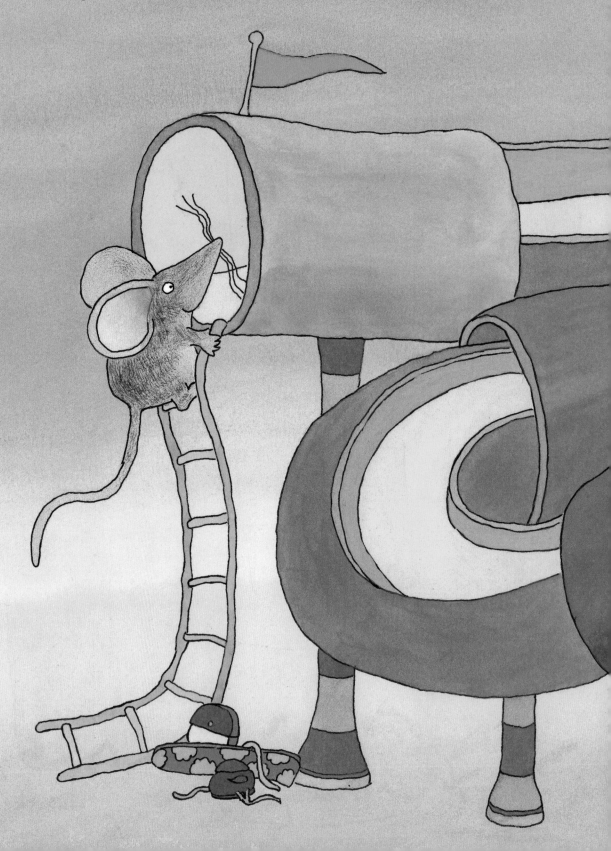

"How will you find her?"

"I'll travel by train."

"I'll travel by plane."

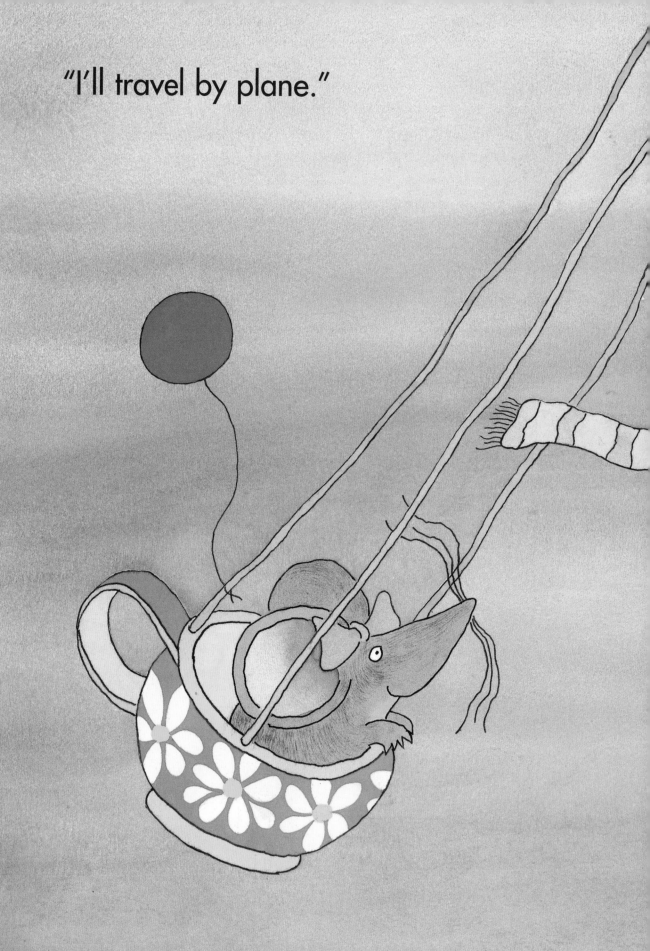

"I'll search on land,
sea, and air
until . . .

I find my mousie fair."

"Aren't you tired?"

"I'm pooped!"

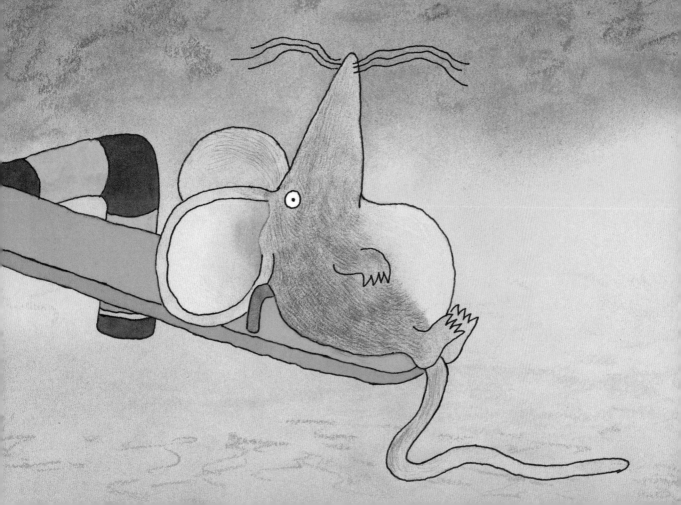

"Isn't it time for supper?"

"Oh, my gosh, I better hurry home!"

"I'm home at last and my feet are sore.

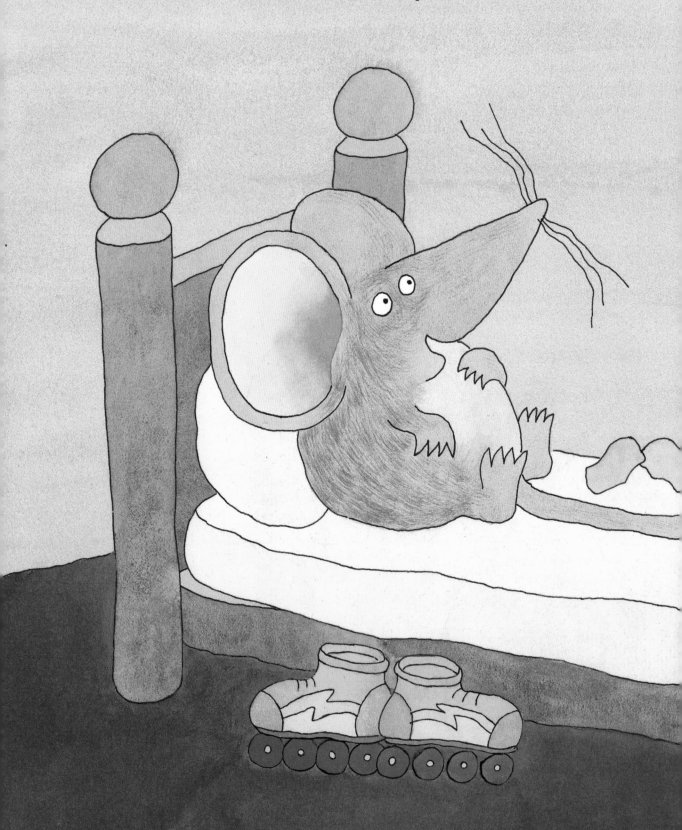

And guess what I've found?"

"What have you found?"

"The mouse I love . . ."

"is the mouse next door!"